THE REEL TRUTH

FISH CAMP COZY MYSTERIES, BOOK 4

SUMMER PRESCOTT

SUMMER PRESCOTT BOOKS PUBLISHING

Copyright 2025 Summer Prescott Books

All Rights Reserved. No part of this publication nor any of the information herein may be quoted from, nor reproduced, in any form, including but not limited to: printing, scanning, photocopying, or any other printed, digital, or audio formats, without prior express written consent of the copyright holder.

**This book is a work of fiction. Any similarities to persons, living or dead, places of business, or situations past or present, is completely unintentional.

CHAPTER ONE

Eugenia Barkley woke to the sound of a boat revving what sounded like a very large motor behind her cabin at the marina. Yawning, she opened her eyes and grinned when she saw sunlight streaming through the sheers that lightly covered her massive bedroom window. She had an amazing view of the cove behind her cabin, and now that spring had sprung, the boaters, fishermen, and even a sprinkling of tourists, were getting out on the lake early, ready to snag a largemouth bass, or just enjoy the sun on their skin and the breeze in their hair.

She had made it. Against all odds, city girl, Eu, as only one of two residents in the entire resort who had stayed put, had made it through an Ozarks winter. The regular appearance of the sun, and the warmer temps that it had brought with it, were a balm to her soul. Eu had more energy, was more productive, and felt much more like smiling, despite her rather frustrating circumstances.

She was still mystified about the mother she never knew, though she'd heard stories from people who knew her that challenged everything she'd always assumed. But she hadn't stopped digging for truth, though she kept hitting nothing but dead ends.

Glancing at her phone, she saw that it was after six o'clock.

"The general store is open," she said with a smile, throwing the covers back and sliding out of bed. "And with any luck, the fish are biting."

Dashing to the kitchen, she pushed the button to start the coffeemaker, then went back to her room to toss on a pair of shorts, flip flops, and a hooded sweatshirt. Spring in the Ozarks was beautiful, but the mornings could be chilly when she got to the fishing hole early.

After downing a cup of coffee in between bites of a lemon blueberry muffin, she poured the rest of the coffee into a thermos and headed for the little store at the top of the hill that led into the resort. Her thighs burned as she reached the top, but she smiled. Exercise felt good. It had been a long, cold winter and just being outside without freezing made Eu feel glad to be alive.

"Morning, Trixie," she sang out, greeting the smoky-voiced, gruff, tattooed proprietor who'd been more than kind to her since she'd arrived, all green and citified, several months ago.

"It's too dang early to be that cheerful, city-slicker," Trixie rasped, good naturedly.

"It's a sunny day, perfect for fishing. All I need are some good minnows and I'll be set. Gotta catch 'em when they're biting." Eu shrugged, grabbing a bag of jerky to snack on. If the fishing was good, she might not get back to the cabin before lunch.

"Speaking of that... You heard from the professor lately?" Trixie waggled her eyebrows, making Eu blush like a teenager as they headed toward the oversized aquarium filled with darting minnows.

"He texted the other day. The new semester started, so he's teaching again," Eu replied, pretending to be suddenly fascinated by a display of bass lures.

"Uh-huh. That's one good-looking man. You better snag that one while the gettin's good," Trixie teased.

"Wait, there's a good-looking man in this place?"

Eu turned at the sound of the lilting voice to see a beautiful blonde woman, who looked familiar somehow, standing behind the counter. Eu looked at Trixie in wonder. No one was ever allowed behind her counter.

"He ain't your type," Trixie replied to the woman. "Besides, I think he may have more than a little bit of interest in this one." She inclined her head toward Eu, who blushed again.

"Is that so?" The woman grinned and came out from behind the counter to join them. She looked at Eu. "You fish?" she asked, eyebrows raised.

"Yep, ever since I was a kid," Eu replied.

"This troublemaker here is my baby sister, Bella," Trixie told Eu, handing her the bucket of minnows.

Eu's mouth dropped open, but she recovered quickly. The two women couldn't be more different, but now that Trixie had mentioned it, she could see the resemblance.

"Hi, Bella. I'm Eu," she introduced herself.

"Wait... What? You're me? I don't understand." Bella frowned.

Eu laughed. "Sorry about that. My name is Eugenia, but everyone calls me Eu."

"I can see why." Bella blinked at her. "Eugenia

sounds like someone's great-grandmother or something."

"See, I told you she was trouble," Trixie said, shaking her head.

"No, it's fine. It is an old-fashioned name, and I think it actually is a family name."

"No offense. I've just never heard of anyone named Eugenia in this century." Bella laughed.

"Don't you have something to do?" Trixie gave her sister a pointed look.

"Nope, I'm on vacation, remember?" Bella replied, taking a big bite out of a Caramel Cluster candy bar. "Oh, this is so good. These things are my favorite."

"Wandering around eating all my inventory…I'm gonna put you to work," Trixie muttered. "If I ate all that candy I wouldn't be able to fit through the door."

Eu handed her some cash for the minnows and her snack and headed for the door. "Nice to meet you, Bella."

"You, too. Good luck!" She waved, her mouth full of Caramel Cluster.

Eu headed down to the fishing hole, smiling and shaking her head as she replayed the interaction. It was crazy to think that Trixie and Bella came from the same family.

Crappie Callie was in her usual spot when Eu arrived, but this time, when Eu gave her a cheery hello, she nodded in response, and Eu could've sworn that she nearly smiled. Nearly. Rome wasn't built in a day.

As had become her custom, now that she'd made some progress with the enigmatic fisherwoman, Eu chattered about her morning and meeting Trixie's sister, Bella, and how nice the weather was. Every once in a while, Callie would raise an eyebrow or nod, so at least she was listening.

Then Eu got a bite. It started out as a light tapping that made the tip of her fishing rod jump just the tiniest bit. Ready to set the hook if the opportunity arose, Eu held tight to the grip, her left hand on the reel.

It hit again. Tap, tap... Tap, tap.

"Come on now, don't be shy," Eu murmured, her eyes glued to the tip of her pole.

Suddenly the tip of the rod bounced so profoundly that Eu nearly dropped it, but she recovered in time to give a quick flick of the wrist and set the hook. Then the battle was on. It seemed that the faster Eu reeled, the harder the fish on the other end of the line tried to dive for the bottom.

Callie got up from her chair and grabbed the net,

ready to scoop up whatever monster happened to be on Eu's line.

"It doesn't feel like it's huge, but it's sure putting up a fight." Eu grunted, struggling to keep the tip of the rod up and reel at the same time.

"Spring crappie," Callie said, nodding sagely.

She was right. A flash of green and golden white belly showed just below the surface of the water right before Callie scooped it up in the net.

"Nice one," she said mildly, when Eu grabbed the good-sized fish by his lower jaw and removed the hook.

"Thanks! And thanks for the help. He's definitely a keeper," Eu replied, holding the fish up to the measuring stick that had been affixed to one of the upright supports of the shack that surrounded the fishing hole.

"Who's a keeper?" a familiar voice asked, making Eu blush and almost caused her to drop her fish before she pulled her keeper basket out of the water.

"Michael! What are you doing here?" Eu asked, grinning from ear to ear and inwardly cringing at how delighted she sounded.

"It's spring break, and I had a craving for fresh air and fishing," the handsome professor replied, holding up his fishing rod, tackle box and bucket of minnows.

He wore plaid cargo shorts and a SPF fishing shirt, and Eu thought he looked adorable. "Hey, Callie," he said, flashing a smile.

Callie nodded. "Michael," she said, watching the tip of her pole.

Eu slipped her crappie into the keeper basket and put it back into the water and was about to speak again when Michael's "Whoa!" startled her.

The tip of Callie's rod had dipped nearly into the water, and she was doing battle with a fish that, if the angle of the rod was any indication, was going to put Eu's crappie to shame. Michael netted a large crappie that was nearly an inch longer than Eu's for Callie and eagerly put his line in the water.

There was very little conversation among them for the next couple of hours. The crappie were hitting hard and fast, and Eu wouldn't have been surprised if they all caught their limit. She had just put down her coffee cup when something hit her line hard.

Grabbing the rod, Eu fought for what seemed like forever. As soon as she reeled in a tiny bit, the fish would dive again. Her arms ached from shoulder to wrist, but there was no way in the world she was going to give up.

Michael picked up the net and stood beside her.

"It's behaving like it might be a bass," he said in a low voice. "Make sure you don't…"

His sentence was interrupted when Eu finally caught sight of the fish, yelped, reeled hard, and pulled up on the tip of her rod. A gorgeous and humongous bass leapt from the water, and as Eu gasped, it flipped and flailed and worked its way off of the hook, leaving Eu's line hanging limply from the end of her pole.

"…let it break the surface of the water," Michael finished his sentence.

"Nooooo!" Eu groaned, her aching shoulders slumping. "Well, I guess that's my cue to clean my fish and go. I have an article I should be working on anyway." She sighed.

"Well, I'm celebrating being on break with a barbeque at five tonight, if you two lovely ladies would like to come by," Michael replied, glancing at Callie and Eu.

"I will never turn down barbeque," Eu said with a grin. "Besides, I won't be able to move my arms enough to cook tonight." She laughed, rubbing her upper arms.

"Great, it's a plan then," Michael replied. "Callie?" She shrugged. "Well, the invitation is open. Drop by if you can."

"What should I bring?" Eu asked.

"Pickles. I can't get enough of those homemade ones, and whatever else you want. There'll be plenty of food."

"Can't wait!" Eu replied, picking up her basket and heading for the cleaning station.

CHAPTER TWO

"Michael and Callie are going to love my potato salad," Eu said with a grin, as she sprinkled in herbs and spices. Her potato salad was legendary among her Los Angeles friends, and she was asked to bring it to every event she attended.

She'd taken her dad's simple, but delicious, recipe of potatoes, mustard, mayo, chopped eggs, and salt and pepper, and had added her own little twists. After mixing the ingredients together, she put the potato salad into a decorative dish, sprinkled a dash of paprika across the top for a bit of color, and snapped a plastic lid on top before placing it in the fridge.

"Now, for impressive dish number two," she said, grabbing a large skillet and placing it on the stove. She took a package of thick-sliced bacon from the refrigerator and chopped half the slices into tiny cubes, then tossed them into the preheated skillet, where they made a delightful sizzle and enticing aroma on impact.

Keeping an eye on the frying bacon, she finely diced half of a sweet Vidalia onion and sprinkled it into the pan with the bacon. The smell that drifted up from the pan was heavenly. She minced and added a clove of garlic, and her stomach growled. When the onions had caramelized and the cubes of bacon were crispy but not overdone, Eu opened a large can of baked beans, drained the bacon fat from the pan and added the beans. As the mixture bubbled, she put in dashes of honey barbecue sauce, ketchup, a touch of molasses, and just a splash of Worcestershire sauce.

"Oh, man. I'm going to have to restrain myself." She chuckled, using a teaspoon to taste the beans. "We'll just see if the way to a man's heart is truly through his stomach." She blushed at the thought and shook her head. "At least I dream big."

She poured the beans into a vintage casserole dish that she was surprised to see in her mother's spotless kitchen, and covered it with a clear glass lid, then placed it into an insulated container in seventies colors of avocado, burnt orange and mustard, that fit the dish exactly.

Hustling to her closet, she selected a figure-hugging sweater and a clean pair of jean capris to wear to the barbecue. She ran a brush through her hair, put on a bit of eyeliner and lip gloss, and headed back to the kitchen for the beans and potato salad.

Eu could smell the barbeque before she even reached Michael's cabin, and when she knocked on the door and Michael opened it, the faint scent of his cologne mixed with the smokiness of the grill nearly had her blushing again.

"Welcome!" he stepped back from the door, beckoning her in.

"Thanks," Eu said, noting that the interior of his cabin was very masculine – sleek and contemporary. "Where should I put these?" She held up the food.

"Just take them straight through to the deck." He nodded toward the sliders. His cabin had the same floor plan as hers but had a very different vibe. It suited him. "The meats are about to come off the grill, so we'll want to dive right in. Do you need serving spoons?" he asked, following her out.

"Nope. I have some in the bag with the potato salad," Eu replied.

Callie was sitting in a deck chair gazing out at the lake when Eu placed the food on the large folding table that Michael had set up along the side rail.

"Hey, Callie," Eu greeted her, shocked that she had actually showed up. Callie nodded once and resumed her inspection of the lake.

"Oh, wow. That cornbread looks amazing. Did you make that too, Michael?" Eu asked, salivating at the sight of it. It had little pieces of jalapeno in it and was topped with a baked cheese crust.

"No, ma'am. Although I'd like to take credit for it, the cornbread and veggie tray are Callie's contribution."

"Nice!" Eu approved, smiling at Callie. "I love both, so thank you in advance."

"Welcome," Callie replied, one corner of her mouth tilting upward ever so slightly. Progress.

"Did you guys catch a ton more fish after I left this morning?" Eu asked, glancing at Callie, then at Michael, who had turned toward the grill and was filling a platter with all kinds of barbecued meat. The smell was amazing, and watching the shift of his broad shoulders under his crisp blue button-down shirt wasn't bad either.

"I left shortly after you did, but I caught this one," Michael said, showing her a massive bass filet on his spatula.

"Yum!" Eu replied. "I'm guessing those are

homemade croutons on the Caesar salad too, aren't they?" she teased.

"Guilty as charged. The texture is better when I make my own." He shrugged. "Alright, ladies, line up for the buffet, grab a plate, and let's dig in."

Eu picked up a plate from the stack on the table and handed it to Callie, then waited for her to go first. Callie took a little bit of everything, as did Eu, then Michael. When they all settled in at the outdoor table, he poured them all a healthy serving of a dangerously delicious red wine. The conversation flowed well, with even Callie commenting every now and again, particularly after a couple of glasses of wine, until all of them sat back in their chairs, stuffed to the gills on amazing food.

"I don't know about you ladies, but I'm going to have to let my food settle a bit before I have any dessert," Michael said, with what looked like a very satisfied exhale.

"Dessert?" Eu groaned, patting her tummy. "I have absolutely no room left for dessert, even though it almost hurts to say that." She laughed.

"Same." Callie nodded.

"It's unanimous then. Why don't you two head down to the firepit with your wine glasses, and I'll put the food away then meet you there with another bottle of wine."

"If you insist." Eu giggled, raising her wine glass, already feeling the effects of her first two drinks.

She and Callie headed toward the firepit that was halfway between the house and the water and settled into a couple of cushion-covered Adirondack chairs, propping their feet up on the rim of the large round firepit, which Michael had lit earlier.

"Here we go," Michael said, appearing a few minutes later and filling their glasses before taking a seat across from them, his back to the lake.

Eu sipped at hers, enjoying the flavor as it rolled across her tongue, but she couldn't help but notice that Callie downed her glass pretty quickly, and held it out to Michael for more.

"This is really good, isn't it, Callie," Eu said, holding up her glass. She figured wine quality might be a non-threatening way to get her reticent neighbor to talk, since she was clearly enjoying it.

Callie gazed over at Eu, lifted her glass and nodded. Then, shockingly, still staring in what looked like a contemplative manner, she spoke.

"Your mother and I were very good friends, you know," Callie said, in a surprisingly quiet and cultured voice that was most unlike her typical grunts and utterances.

"Oh?" Eu said softly, trying not to let her reaction show. Her heart thrummed in her chest, and she looked at Callie as though the legendary fisherwoman was a timid deer that might bolt into the woods at any moment if Eu said or did the wrong thing.

"You look exactly like her. The first time I saw you, I thought I was seeing a ghost." Callie took a gulp of wine and shook her head.

Eu marveled at how refined her speech was. In a matter of moments, a tough old cabin-dweller had turned into what sounded very much like a woman of substance. Had her gruff exterior been an act all along?

She didn't know what to say, so she stayed quiet, while Callie continued to stare at her.

"We met when we were young. I was doing a modeling shoot on the Riviera, and she was there with her sister. They were on break from university. We were all young and free – the way people are before life and other people's expectations bring them down." Callie smiled sadly. "It probably surprises you that I was a model."

Eu shook her head. "No, I knew that because Fran recognized you from a vintage surfing ad."

Callie's brows rose, and she took another sip of wine. "Wow, she has a good eye. My life was so wonderfully uncomplicated back then. Until my parents decided that I needed to settle down with a boring young man from a good family. I went through all the motions, hating every second of it. China patterns, invitations, menus." She shuddered. "All that work to permanently chain myself to a man that I didn't even like, much less love."

"So, what did you do?" Eu murmured, wide-eyed. She couldn't help herself. Callie had turned into an entirely different person, right before her eyes.

"The night before the wedding, when everyone went back to their hotel rooms to sleep off the food and booze, I took all my money out of my bank account and trust fund, which my parents had released since I was getting married, and I got as far away from New York as I possibly could. I came here, paid cash for my cabin, and disappeared. I met a farm boy along the way and had a daughter that I gave up – you met her – Clarissa. That's my only regret, giving her up. From what I heard, her dad was killed in a car accident, and she was raised by her grandparents. Nice couple," Callie said sadly.

"I'm so sorry you had to go through that," Eu

said, as Michael silently topped off both of their glasses again.

"Leaving my fiancé and my family was the best decision I ever made. And while it crushed me to give away my baby girl, I had zero ability to raise a child, particularly alone. My mother didn't teach me much, I was closer to my nannies than to her." Callie shrugged.

"But my mother found you here?" Eu asked, frowning.

"Definitely not. I knew that she was in the same situation, because we'd kept in touch, and I told her where I was. Poor kid. She didn't run like I did. She got married to a man she didn't love and kept a place here for when she needed to escape."

Eu swallowed hard. "But… Why didn't she just stay with my dad, then? Was it my fault?" she asked.

"I thought so, at first. I blamed you for ruining the life she could have had, because I figured that she was like I was and just wasn't ready to settle down and raise a family. She was so talented and vivacious when she was here, but whenever we spoke on the phone and she was at home, it was like she had no spirit. She loved you and your dad with every part of her heart and soul. When you were really little, your dad would come down here with you, and your mom was beyond thrilled."

Eu's eyes welled with tears. All these years, she'd thought such awful things about her mother. That she'd callously abandoned her. "Why did we stop visiting her? Why didn't I ever get the chance to know her?" she asked, as two tears streaked slowly down her cheeks.

"I thought your dad kept you away, and I could never understand why. That's why I was so awful to you when you first arrived here. I thought you hadn't cared a bit about how much your mother had been yearning to see you and that you were only here to collect your inheritance. Then I did some digging recently." Callie bit her lip and gave Eu what looked like a deeply contrite look.

"And?" Eu took a sip of wine that caught in her throat for a moment before sliding down.

"And I found out that your mother's husband was an awful human being. He found out that you and your dad had been visiting, and he threatened to destroy you and your dad both if you returned, so as much as your dad loved your mom, he kept you away to keep you safe. Your mom showed me a painting that she did of you and your dad the last time she saw you. Your dad led you away and you kept looking back at your mom, crying and wanting to go to her. It was heartbreaking."

A sob caught in Eu's throat, and she drew in a deep shuddering breath, her tears flowing more freely. "I've seen that painting. I thought she only knew me from the pictures she had. I guess my dad must've sent them to her." Eu bit her lower lip and closed her eyes, trying to maintain her composure.

"No, honey. That would have been too risky. He didn't send them to her. He sent them to me, and I gave them to her, even though I knew they'd make her cry. If he had sent them to her and had been intercepted by her husband, it wouldn't have been good for any of you."

"Did he have mob ties?" Michael asked quietly, from the other side of the fire pit.

"Something like that." Callie nodded.

Michael got up and headed toward the house.

"If I had only known…" Eu shook her head.

"You couldn't have known. Your dad took that to his grave with him. When your mom found out he'd passed, she was like a ghost, drifting in and out of her cabin, not eating, always wiping her tears. She would've been so proud of the woman you've become," Callie said kindly.

"Thank you," Eu replied, swiping away her tears and taking deep breaths.

"Who wants cake?" Michael broke the pall that had settled around the fire pit.

Callie smiled, and Eu chuckled, glad for the moment of comic relief.

"Is that even a question?" she asked, her voice still husky with tears.

"None for me, thanks," Callie said, standing a bit unsteadily, but balancing herself in short order. "I've gotta watch this girlish figure." She grinned.

Eu stared at her for a moment, then got up and gave her a hug. Much to her surprise, Callie hugged her back.

"Oh!" Eu drew back, shocked that when she hugged Callie, there was a tiny woman beneath what had to be multiple layers of clothes.

Callie laughed. "It's all a disguise. I don't look like this when I'm not out in public." She patted her frayed and shapeless sweatshirt. "All these years of hiding, I guess."

"You shouldn't hide," Eu said quietly, moving in for another hug.

"Old habits die hard," Callie said simply and turned to go.

"Do you want me to walk you back to your cabin?" Eu asked.

"Nope. You go on and eat your cake with the professor. All the critters around here are more scared of me than I am of them." Her back hills accent and manner returned in a flash.

Eu sat back down and stared at the firepit, her head whirling. Michael came over and handed her a piece of the most luscious looking chocolate layer cake she'd ever seen, then sat down in the chair next to her that Callie had just vacated.

"Learn something new every day, huh?" he said softly, digging his fork into his cake and watching Eu while he chewed.

"Yeah. Wow." At a loss for words, Eu shook her head, still focused on the fire. "Did you know any of this?"

Michael swallowed. "No. I knew the two of them were great friends. When they got together, it was all laughter and giggles and mischief. Then Randi would go back home, and Callie would disappear into her shell again. After your mom passed, she hasn't been the same."

Eu slid her fork into her cake and took a sizable bite, savoring it as she digested what she'd heard. "How on earth do you make the best baked goods on the planet?" she asked, when the burst of chocolatey goodness hit her tongue. "Seriously, it's perfect."

Michael laughed. "It's a hobby. I enjoy making things."

"And you're a perfectionist," Eu teased, putting her hand in front of her mouth to speak as she chewed.

"Guilty as charged," he replied, setting his now-empty plate aside.

"Well, I for one, am glad that your hobby is baking. How long is your spring break?" Eu asked, then popped the last bite of cake into her mouth.

"Why, wanting to stock up on cookies before I go back?" Michael teased.

Before she could think twice, and likely due to the wine she'd consumed, Eu replied honestly. "Nope. I like your company as well as your baked goods," she said, giving him a dreamy smile.

"Well, I can stay here for a bit longer than my actual spring break, because I can teach remotely, so I'm just playing it by ear," he replied.

Eu couldn't tell if it was the wine, the cake, or the look that Michael was giving her that made her feel warm and relaxed from her head to her toes. Maybe all three?

"Good, you should stay for quite a while then,"

she proclaimed, rising just as unsteadily from her chair as Callie had, and not recovering nearly as quickly. She giggled. "This was the best. I loved it. But I think I should go home now."

Michael was at her elbow in a flash, steadying her. "How about I walk you to your door and scare the bears away?" He grinned.

"I feel safer already," Eu replied with a wide smile, enjoying the feel of his hand on her elbow. "Well, this is me," she said, when they stepped up onto her porch. "Thank you for dinner and cake." The world was beginning to tilt in the most wonderful way, and she couldn't help but admire Michael's dimples. She reached up to touch one. "You are so handsome." Eu tilted her head back and gazed up at him.

"You're too kind," Michael said.

Eu felt as though his eyes were looking directly into her soul and that he liked what he saw.

"Naw, I'm not being kind. It's true. I'm glad you came for spring break. I like you," Eu proclaimed, swaying a bit.

Michael reached out to steady her again, chuckling. "The feeling is mutual," he said.

Eu fell into his arms, and he hugged her briefly, then held her at arm's length, examining her carefully.

"Are you going to be okay?" he asked.

Eu's head spun a bit. "I'm a little sleepy," she said, pursing her lips.

"Do you want me to help you inside?"

"Yep," Eu replied, her forehead dropping down onto his chest. "You smell amazing."

"Okay, let's get you inside," Michael said.

He swung her up into his arms, carried her inside, and lowered her gently to the sofa, placing a throw pillow under her head. Her eyelids felt so heavy, and his voice seemed to come to her from a great distance.

"I'll be right back," he said, heading toward the kitchen.

He returned moments later, but to Eu, who was struggling to stay awake, it felt like an eternity. She saw him place a huge bowl by the end of the sofa, just in case, and he brought a straw to her lips, encouraging her to take a sip of ice cold water, then placed the water bottle on the coffee table, where she could reach it. The last thing she remembered was the warm and cuddly feeling of being covered with a soft quilt.

CHAPTER THREE

Eu's eyes felt grainy, and her throat was parched when she woke up in the dark, not quite aware of where she was. She sat up and finally realized that she'd been sleeping on her couch. Her phone was in the front pocket of the hoodie that she'd been wearing since yesterday and when she took it out, she saw that it was only five thirty.

"What time did I go to sleep last night?" she wondered aloud, frowning. "I need coffee."

She started a pot of coffee, then went to her room and took a quick shower, dressing casually in denim shorts and a cable-knit sweater. After enjoying a cup of coffee while staring out at the lake, which was barely visible in the pre-dawn light, Eu decided to go for a hike to clear her head a bit. She didn't have a headache, but she felt a bit lethargic.

Taking her water bottle with her, she headed up the hill toward the general store, turning onto a path that led into the woods behind the marina. She had a flashlight on a lanyard around her neck that was helping to light the path in front of her until the sun rose a bit higher, and she took deep breaths of fresh, cool, morning air.

Just as the sun made it possible to turn off her flashlight because she could see the path in front of her, a gunshot rang out and a bloodcurdling scream shattered the stillness of the woods ahead of her and Eu froze, her heart thudding in her chest.

"Holy moly. Someone needs help," she gasped, setting terror aside out of concern.

She took off running through the trees, toward the place where the scream had seemed to come from and stopped short when she saw a tree with what looked like fresh blood on it. Turning on her phone's flashlight, Eu took a closer look and determined that the stain on the tree was definitely blood. While her flashlight worked, her cell phone was out of range and had no reception.

"I have to get back to the marina and call the police," she murmured, scanning the woods around her and hoping she didn't meet the same fate as the person who'd shed blood on the tree.

Adrenaline crashing through her, Eu ran as fast as she could back down the path, only coming to a stop when she emerged from the woods and the bars on her phone returned. She quickly dialed 911 and was told to stay where she was and wait for a patrol car.

"I really hope they send out someone other than Carter and Writman." Eu sighed, in no mood to deal with two deputies who had chips on their shoulders, one much more so than the other.

Eu sat on a picnic table near the marina and waited, scrolling through her phone trying to distract herself from what she'd just seen. When she heard the crunch of tires on gravel, she turned and saw what she'd feared – Carter and Writman were answering the call.

"Miss me?" she asked, with a wan smile.

"You made a report of an attack," Writman said.

"I mean, yeah, that's what it seemed like," Eu replied.

"Why don't you lead us to the site where you think it happened, and you can tell us everything on the way," Carter, the more reasonable of the two, suggested.

She found her way back to the tree with the blood on it and pointed it out to them.

Carter squatted down and turned on his flashlight for a closer look. He nodded, then looked up at Eu. "Since you heard a gunshot and a scream, it may have been an animal. Lots of 'em out here sound like a woman screaming when they're hurt," he explained. "But we'll check it out."

"Probably ain't never been hunting before, have ya, city girl?" Writman said, his lip curling in a manner that could only mean contempt.

"Gross, no. And I never will." Refusing to be baited into a hostile response, she turned back to Carter. "You need me for anything else?" she asked.

"No, ma'am. We'll be in touch if we need anything else," Carter replied, taking a swab of the blood.

"And you can bet we'll figure out if you've been up to any funny business," Writman drawled.

"Oh, give me a break." Eu rolled her eyes, exasperated, and stalked off toward the marina.

CHAPTER FOUR

"I can't believe those two. This is what I get for being a good citizen," Eu muttered, stomping toward the fishing hole. When she got there, she stood staring. The woman who was sitting in Callie's chair didn't look very much like the Callie she'd seen for the past several months, but it was her. The leather bracelet that Eu's mother, Miranda, had made for her was on her wrist.

Gone was the messy gray hair that perpetually looked like it hadn't been washed in days. The skin that had seemed wrinkled and dry now glowed with natural color, and what had looked like a shapeless figure had been revealed to be impressive once Callie had donned clothing that actually fit. A shiny ponytail poked out of the back of a sporty fishing hat.

"Wow, you look amazing!" Eu marveled, trying not to gawk at the transformation.

"Amazing what a little moisturizer will do, and someone told me that I needed to stop hiding." Callie chuckled. "You look frazzled."

"I am. Did you hear a gunshot and a scream this morning, just around dawn?" Eu asked.

"I sure did. Made the hair on the back of my neck stand up." Callie nodded.

"I called the sheriff's department and Tweedle-dee and Tweedle-dum came to check it out. They said what I heard could have been an animal." Eu sighed, shaking her head.

"No way. That definitely did not sound like an animal," Callie replied. "I also heard a big boat pull into the marina real slow and quiet right before that. I stood up to look at it, because there usually isn't anyone out on the water that early at this time of year. I can't remember the name on the side, but I think it had something to do with a bird. It was only there for a few minutes then it left just as quietly as it had come in."

Eu frowned. "That sounds pretty odd."

Callie shook her head. "Nah, it's actually not that unusual, they probably just went to get supplies from the store."

"Yeah, could be," Eu agreed, making a mental note to walk up to the store and ask Trixie if she'd had any particularly early customers after she was done with her morning fishing. She needed to stare at a pole and concentrate on catching a fish to calm her nerves a bit.

When she wasn't watching her pole, Eu was gazing at the doorway of the fishing hole, hoping to see Michael walking jauntily down the path to the marina, but he didn't make an appearance before she started getting bites, so she turned her attention back to the reason that she was there and caught a couple of fish.

Leaving her catch in the keeper basket, Eu headed up to the general store to talk to Trixie and was dismayed to find the typically calm cool shopkeeper in a tizzy.

"Trixie, what's wrong?" Eu asked, when she entered the shop and saw Trixie sitting behind the counter, her head in her hands.

"It's that durn fool sister of mine. She's gone missing," Trixie replied, scanning the windows as she spoke. "Ain't seen her since last night when she went to bed."

Eu's pulse raced. She didn't want to unduly worry

Trixie, but she told her about what she'd seen and heard that morning.

"I hope some dang hunter didn't mistake my greenhorn sister for a deer out there." Trixie crossed her arms and grimaced.

Eu was so distressed at the news that she entirely forgot to ask Trixie whether or not she'd had any early morning customers. "Carter and Writman are on the case, but I'll try to figure out anything I can."

Thinking hard on the walk back to the cabin, Eu couldn't even decide where to start on an investigation. Her furrowed brow relaxed, however, when she saw a basket sitting on her porch with a note on it.

It smelled delightful and when she pulled back a corner of the cloth to peek at what was inside, she saw a variety of muffins and pastries.

Thought you might want a little pick-me-up this morning. Enjoy! M

CHAPTER FIVE

Munching on a chocolate chip muffin while drinking her second cup of coffee, Eu turned the morning's events over and over in her mind. Worry churned in her stomach, and she hoped that Bella's disappearance, the gunshot, and the blood in the woods weren't related. When she finished her breakfast, she stared out at the lake without seeing it, tapping her fingers on the table.

"Maybe the deputies are gone, and I can go take another look," she mused. "It's worth a shot," Eu muttered, cringing when she realized what she'd just said. "Or hopefully not a shot." She sighed and headed for the front door.

Eu moved as soundlessly through the woods as she could, taking the same path that she'd been on, and hoping that the deputies were gone so she could take a better look around now that it was full-on daylight outside.

It was a gorgeous day, with blue skies and lots of sunshine, but Eu still felt shivers of apprehension up and down her spine as she walked. Something had happened in those woods, something that had caused bleeding.

Every time she heard faint sounds of what she hoped were birds and squirrels moving through the woods, intent upon their business, Eu's heart slammed in her chest as she paused, staring in whatever direction from which the sounds had come. But she pressed on. Trixie's sister might be out there somewhere.

When she came around the bend, Eu breathed a sigh of relief. The deputies were gone. They'd probably laughed at her when she left, thinking she was making a fuss about the circle of life that didn't faze them at all. But Eu wasn't so sure that foul play hadn't been involved.

She peered closely at the blood on the tree and saw that a piece of bark was missing. Hopefully that meant that Carter and Writman had taken a decent sample. Scanning the ground in the immediate vicinity, she saw another drop of blood on some leaves that were roughly six feet up the hill from the tree. A few feet beyond that was another. Then another. Eu followed the trail and when she glanced up, her heart pounded in her throat.

The trail seemed to head toward a house at the top of the hill. Unlike the gorgeous mansions that were usually built atop hills and bluffs in the Ozarks, this house was small and had paint peeling from the graying wooden siding. All the windows facing the lake were blocked by curtains or yellowing shades, which seemed extremely odd. It didn't look abandoned, but it did look ominous.

Eu stopped and swallowed hard, fear tickling at the base of her spine. "I have to go up there. Bella could be in there," she whispered, the sound of her voice out of place in the stillness of the woods. "In for a penny, in for a pound," she muttered, taking long strides up the hill before she could change her mind.

She rapped hard on the door, her knuckles scraping against the rough wood. While she waited for an answer, she dropped her gaze to the cement stoop and noticed that a dribble of blood had slid down one of the steps. Her heart raced, and just as she considered whether or not to turn tail and run, the door flew open, revealing an angry man who reeked of onions and stale beer.

He stood just under six feet, which still made Eu feel small and defenseless, and had at least a week's worth of beard stubble with dirty strands of hair that had flopped across his furrowed brow.

"What you want, girl?" he growled, glaring at Eu. His breath could only be described as malevolent, but she somehow managed not to wince.

"Hi! A friend of mine went for a walk this morning and she doesn't know the woods very well, so I think she might be lost, and I wondered if you might have seen her," Eu said brightly, with a smile like sunshine. Maybe she could 'kill him with kindness.'

"Ain't seen nobody and wouldn't tell ya if I did."

The man moved to shut the door, but Eu put her foot on the threshold and moved forward. "I'm sorry," she said, her face growing stiff from maintaining a fake pleasant expression. "But I couldn't help but notice that there's a little spot of blood on your porch. Are you okay?" she asked, catching a glimpse of the bleak interior of the house. It seemed as grey inside as it was outside.

"You ain't from around here, girl." He narrowed his eyes in an even more hostile glare.

Eu shook her head. "Not exactly, no."

"Then you don't know how things work here in

the hills. You best mind your business," he said, his tone menacing. "As long as you're standing on my porch, you're trespassing, and ain't nothing good ever happened to a trespasser in these parts, so you just get on outta here and don't come back, ya hear?" he ordered.

When Eu stepped back in surprise, he slammed the door in her face. "Well, that went well," she muttered, heading back down the trail much faster than she'd come up.

When Eu came out of the woods, thankful that she hadn't encountered anything, or anyone, scary along the way, she went down to the fishing hole to see if Michael or Callie might know the identity of the man in the house.

She was frustrated and disappointed that neither one of them was fishing but figured out her next move on the walk back to her cabin.

"I know how to use technology. I'm going to look up his house on Property Finder and get his name," she vowed. "Something tells me that he probably has a very interesting past."

CHAPTER SIX

"Josiah Hessel," Eu murmured aloud, when she discovered the identity of the man who owned the house on the hill. "Let's see what we can find out about you." She focused intently on the computer screen. "Whoa, he's my age. I thought he was at least ten years older."

She scrolled through what little information she could find, but didn't find anything of consequence. He'd had a few run-ins with law enforcement, but didn't seem to be a hardened criminal. Then she found a restraining order against him that had been filed a while back by someone who had the same last name as Trixie.

"Time to go to the store," Eu said, closing her laptop.

She strode up the hill, the muscles in her calves feeling the results of her fairly strenuous hike earlier. Trixie was sitting in her usual spot behind the counter, but instead of thumbing through one of her many outdoorsy magazines, she had her arms crossed and was staring blankly into space.

"No word yet?" Eu asked.

"Nothing," Trixie replied, sounding defeated.

"I've been looking into a couple of things, and I have a question. Josiah Hessel lives in the woods right near where I thought I heard a scream. The deputies checked everything out and think it was probably just an animal noise, but I figured I might as well check it out, and when I spoke to Josiah, he was really rude. I couldn't help but wonder if he was hiding something. Or someone," Eu explained gently.

"Josiah Hessel. That's a name I haven't heard in quite a while. Yeah, he lives like a hermit up in that house. Don't take it personally, I don't think he's ever had a kind word to say to anyone ever." Trixie made a face.

"Well, when I looked him up, I noticed that there was a restraining order against him from someone named Ernie Schmidt and I wondered if there might be a connection between you and Ernie," Eu said.

"Ugh. There's another name I never really wanted to hear again. Ernie is my ex. He and Josiah used to be drinking buddies until they had a fight about something. Josiah made some threats, so Ernie went to the sheriff, but between you and me, I don't think Josiah ever would've followed through on the threats. He just liked to talk big." Trixie waved a hand dismissively.

"Is your ex still around here? Do you think he might be involved in Bella's disappearance?" Eu asked.

"Heck no. Ernie wouldn't have the gumption, even though he always had a crush on poor Bella. Trust me, if he would have had to do anything that involved getting his lazy behind off his couch, it wouldn't have happened."

"Are you sure? Maybe he did something to get back at you?" Eu proposed.

Trixie shook her head. "Nah, he ain't got it in him to do real harm, other than emotional, I don't think. Look honey, I appreciate you trying to help and all, but I talked to the sheriff, and he said they'd take care of it, so we should probably just let them. I don't want to be responsible for you getting hurt or disappearing too."

Eu nodded, but Trixie's words had done nothing

to deter her. "Did Bella have any enemies?" she asked.

Trixie smiled sadly and shook her head. "Nope, that girl is as pure as the driven snow, and everyone everywhere has loved her for her entire life. She never meets a stranger and can charm the socks off of every man who ever lived. She's just one of those naturally good people, ya know?"

Eu gave Trixie what she hoped was a reassuring smile. "Yeah, she was very sweet. Well, I'm going to head out now. I'll let you know if I figure anything out," she promised.

"Stay away from it, Eugenia. We don't know what we're dealing with yet," Trixie warned.

"I'll be careful. Take care, Trixie. I'm just down the hill if you want company."

"Thanks hon," Trixie called out as Eu reached the door.

Eu went back to the cabin and made herself a leftover meatloaf sandwich to munch on while she did some research. "Let's see if pure and sweet Bella has any skeletons in her closet," she mused, typing Trixie's sister's name into the search bar.

Scrolling through articles about beauty pageants Bella had won, honors she'd received in school, and charity work that she'd done after moving away from the Ozarks, Eu found an entry from the sheriff's department's daily listing in the newspaper. Bella had filed a lawsuit against a man who was found guilty of stalking her. She'd won the suit, and after more digging, Eu discovered that the man had relocated to another state.

"I wonder if he still lives in that state, or if he might be following Bella wherever she goes," Eu said, the thought giving her a chill. "I'll definitely dig into this one a bit more."

She saved the information that was available from the lawsuit and had just clicked on another entry when there was a loud knock at her door. Her heart leapt, hoping Michael might be bringing over a freshly baked treat to share, but when she opened the door, unfortunately, she was greeted by the grim faces of Carter and Writman.

CHAPTER SEVEN

"Does your patrol car just naturally head for my driveway every time it leaves the lot?" Eu asked.

"We have a few questions for you," Carter replied as Writman stared at her with the expressionless eyes of a shark on the hunt.

"Of course you do. Come on in," she said, flipping her laptop closed as she passed by the kitchen counter, where she'd been sitting. "Coffee?" she asked. There was no sense in antagonizing them. They'd probably deem it suspicious behavior and stay longer.

"No, thanks," Carter replied politely.

"What were you doing up in the woods that early in the morning, and how did you just happen to find blood when it was still pretty dark out there?"

Writman demanded, standing even when his partner sat on the sofa.

"I told you already. I was going for a hike. I like to get exercise out of the way early so that I can get on with my day, and I use a flashlight so I don't trip over anything or run into snakes or something." Eu shuddered at the thought.

"Ain't no snakes out that early in the morning," Writman retorted. "They don't come out until the sun does this time of year."

"Wait a minute," Eu said, eyes narrowing. "You thought the blood that I found was from an animal. A hunting thing. No big deal. But I'm guessing since you're here, that's not the case."

"How would you know that?" Writman shot back.

Eu spoke very slowly and with exaggerated inflection, explaining as if to a five-year-old. "Because you wouldn't bother coming to ask me questions if the blood had been from an animal, which means it must've been human. Do you know whose it is?" she turned to Carter and asked.

"We're not going to comment on an ongoing investigation," Writman replied, before his partner could speak.

In that moment, Eu decided that since they weren't sharing info, she wouldn't either, so she kept the fact that she'd found a blood trail leading to the house on top of the hill to herself.

"Look, I know you've provided some valuable assistance in some of our cases in the past, but right now we'd really appreciate it if you'd just be a good citizen and let us handle things," Carter said, seeming frustrated with his partner.

Eu nodded, wondering why Writman seemed so paranoid all of a sudden and why Carter had made his request so politely.

"Sorry. I've told you everything I did this morning. I hope you figure out what happened," she replied. It was true. She had told them everything she did in the morning, during her hike. They'd never asked her what she'd done since then.

"Keep your nose in your own business this time," Writman said, giving her a dark look as they headed for the door.

"Rude," she replied, resisting the urge to make an unkind gesture toward the prickly deputy.

Eu closed the door behind them after they left and went straight to her laptop to do another search. It seemed awfully odd they'd appeared on her doorstep shortly after she'd spoken to Josiah, so she put his name, along with Carter and Writman into her search bar.

And found a photo of a family reunion, with a couple of familiar local faces in it.

"Bingo," she whispered. After reading the article, she discovered that Josiah Hessel was Deputy Writman's distant cousin. "Well now, isn't that just interesting? No wonder he was being so defensive."

Knowing she should be writing an article for her freelancing gig but being realistic enough to admit that she'd be way too distracted at the moment to produce anything worth reading, Eu decided to head down to the fishing hole. Sometimes staring at the end of the rod, waiting for it to twitch with a bite, worked wonders on her ability to focus. She'd thought through quite a few difficult things while fishing and hoped she might get some clarity regarding Bella's disappearance.

Callie, who looked amazing in a brightly colored top and denim capris, gave Eu a slight smile when she said hello.

"Anything biting?" Eu asked, opening her bucket of minnows.

"Yep, got a good haul so far," Callie replied.

"I came down earlier to see if you or Michael were around, but no one was here," Eu said, just to make conversation.

"I was getting my hair cut," Callie replied, taking

off her fishing hat and shaking gorgeous chestnut curls, laced with grey, free.

"Wow, it looks amazing." Eu grinned.

"Thanks. I feel more like myself than I have in years. Oh, and before I forget again, I wanted to tell you that I remembered the name of the big boat that came into the marina. It had The Sandpiper written on the side."

"The Sandpiper," Eu repeated, baiting her hook. "Good to know. Thanks, Callie."

CHAPTER EIGHT

Eu's gaze looked as though it was directed at the tip of her pole, but her mind was a million miles away. Josiah Hessel. Trixie's ex. Writman. The Sandpiper. She turned the information over and over in her mind trying to make heads or tails of it.

"Are you going to catch that fish or just let him take off with your pole?" Callie asked, startling Eu from her reverie.

She looked over to see her pole bending profoundly toward the water and hurriedly picked it up.

"That doesn't look like a crappie bite," Callie commented, grabbing the net and standing by Eu's side as she battled the fish. "I think you've got yourself a bass on that hook, so make sure you keep that tip up and don't let him break the surface, or he'll be gone."

"Gotcha." Eu grunted, reeling with all her might and grinning at the thrill of it.

Sure enough, when Callie dipped the net into the water and netted the fish, it was a large bass that was so heavy Eu had to hold it in both hands to get it into the keeper basket.

"Whew," she said, cleaning her hands with a baby wipe. "After that, I think I'm going to call it a day and finally go get my latest article done," Eu announced.

"Some days one and done is the way to go," Callie replied, setting the hook and reeling in a good sized crappie.

Eu had every intention of writing her latest article. She really did. But the moment she opened her laptop, the name that Callie had mentioned seemed to call out to her. A bazillion times. Sandpiper. Sandpiper. Sandpiper.

With a sigh, she clicked out of the document she was supposed to be working on and entered The Sandpiper and Ozarks in the search box.

She found several references to its owner, a wealthy local named Nigel Morence, who seemed to have an outstanding reputation as a philanthropist and master fisherman. She checked police reports, the complaints section of the paper, and every other resource she could find, but came up with nothing but glowing references for the hometown hero.

"Nothing to see here," Eu said, re-opening her document. "He was probably just scoping out bass spots for his next tournament."

For the next hour, she worked on her article in earnest, finally taking a break when her stomach growled, reminding her to eat. She whipped up a quick fettuccini Alfredo, with fresh cream, butter, and loads of parmesan cheese, lacing it with just a whisper of basil.

"Oh, this is ridiculous," she moaned, her eyes practically rolling back in her head when she took the first delectable bite. She scrolled through her phone, catching up on the news while she ate, and after she finished, she loaded the dishwasher and poured a glass of wine.

"I'll get this article finished now that my stomach stopped distracting me," she said, chuckling as she opened her laptop.

Eu had just set down her wine glass on the coffee table when she heard a knock at her door.

"Seriously? I have zero patience to deal with

Carter and Writman tonight," she muttered, heading for the foyer.

She knew she had a sour look on her face when she went to the door, but when she saw who was on the other side, her face lit up in delight.

"Hey, did I catch you at a bad time?" Michael asked, carrying a covered dish. "You had a pretty profound scowl when you opened the door."

Eu laughed. "That's because I thought you were the deputy dawgs," she replied. "Come on in."

"Thanks." He smiled, flashing those killer dimples, and Eu's knees felt like jelly.

"What's in the dish?" she asked, waggling her eyebrows.

"I didn't know if you liked them, but I made lemon bars, so I brought some over to see if you wanted them," Michael replied, uncovering the mouthwatering treat with a flourish.

"Lemon bars are one of my favorite desserts," Eu said, gazing down at the luscious looking treats.

"Why limit yourself? They're great for breakfast too," Michael teased.

"Absolutely. Do you want to have some with me?" Eu asked, gesturing toward the deck.

"I ate four before I brought them over," he

confessed, placing a hand over his flat stomach. "But I did want to ask you something."

"Oh?" Eu said, leaning against the kitchen counter and taking a bite. "Oh, my gosh. These are decadent," she gasped, putting a hand in front of her mouth to hide her chewing.

"Thanks, I'm glad you like them."

"I don't like them. I love them," Eu declared. "So, what did you need to ask me?"

"Oh." Michael cleared his throat and stuck his hands in the pockets of his jeans. "Well, I know how much you love animals, so I was wondering if you want to go to the safari park with me tomorrow."

Eu's brows rose. "Safari Park?" she asked.

"Yeah, it's not too far away from here, and they have exotic animals that are kept in natural habitats, so they feel like they're at home. It's pretty cool and I have VIP tickets to the sloth experience, so if you'd like, you can hold and feed a baby sloth and get a behind the scenes tour of the park," Michael explained.

Eu swallowed and hopped up and down, clapping her hands. "Oh, my gosh! I've always wanted to see a sloth," she exclaimed, her voice squeaking with excitement.

"I thought you might enjoy that." Michael grinned. "I'll see you tomorrow."

"See ya!" Eu said, entirely unable to wipe the ear-to-ear smile from her face.

She walked Michael to the door and closed it after him, then leaned against it, her heart thumping in the best possible way.

CHAPTER NINE

Eu sat back in a chair on her deck talking to Fran, her bestie in California, on the phone. She'd told her about hearing the gunshot and the scream, and everything that had happened since.

"I'm sorry, Eu, I know you love that whole outdoorsy thing, and you want to find out more about your mom, but I really think you should consider getting the heck out of the Ozarks once and for all. There are way too many weird things happening out there," Fran insisted.

"It all sounds worse than it really is," Eu said, crossing her fingers. "I just stumble into some odd situations, and I feel like if I can help then I should help. Besides, I really feel like I'm going to have a breakthrough in finding more information about my mom. Callie opened up a little bit, and I learned quite a bit. Also, I have a bit of fun news."

"Oh? Do tell!" Fran replied. Eu could hear the smile in her voice.

"Michael has VIP tickets to a safari park and we're going today. I get to hold and feed a baby sloth," Eu said, squeaking just like she had when Michael had invited her.

"And now we know the real reason why you want to stay in the Ozarks for a bit," Fran teased. "He really knows the way to your heart, doesn't he? He's hitting it out of the park on your first date."

Eu blushed. "It's not a date," she protested, laughing.

"Uh-huh, sure. What time are you supposed to be going?" Fran asked.

Eu glanced at the clock on the microwave and her stomach did a flip-flop. "Oh, no. Fran, I gotta go get ready!"

"I want to hear everything when you get back, got it?" Fran replied.

"Yes ma'am." Eu giggled.

She hit the End button on her phone and hurried back to her bedroom to get ready for the trip.

"Yikes… What do I even wear to a safari park?" she wondered, gazing at the neatly organized clothes in her walk-in closet. "It's supposed to be pretty warm today, so maybe my khaki shorts with a white sleeveless polo shirt. Now shoes. If it's dusty out there, I won't want sandals, but I think tennis shoes will be too casual," she muttered. "Ah, here we go! Ballet flats work for every occasion, and they match my shorts."

Not wanting to look like she was trying too hard, Eu curled the ends of her hair and put it up in a jaunty ponytail, then carefully applied just a touch of eyeliner and a bit of tinted lip gloss. Satisfied with her look, she picked up her purse and heard Michael knock at the front door.

"Whew, just in the nick of time," she whispered, hurrying toward the foyer.

"Wow, you look great," Michael said, leading her to his car and opening her door.

"That's just because you usually see me in fishing clothes with scales in my hair." Eu chuckled, getting into the car and thanking him for holding the door.

"That may be true, but you can totally pull off that look," he teased.

They chatted as they drove to the park, and when Eu saw the sign for the entrance, she sat up straight in her seat, trying to see through the slats of the tall wooden enclosure.

"Do they have dinosaurs in there? It's giving me a bit of a Jurassic Park vibe," Eu said.

"Who knows? This is Missouri." Michael chuckled.

They were met at the gate by a tour guide who showed them where to park and joined them as they got out of the car. After a Jeep ride through the park, with the tour guide stopping and allowing them to meet many of the animals face to face, they were taken to the main building where they were able to help prepare the food for a variety of animals and take it into the enclosures, accompanied by their friendly guide.

On their way back to the room that housed the sloth nursery, where they'd be able to hold and feed baby sloths, they passed an open office door where, unexpectedly, Eu saw a familiar face.

"Benz?" she said, peeking into the office.

"Eugenia, great to see you," Benz said coming over to shake her hand. He turned to Michael.

"Aren't you that professor guy?" he asked.

"Yep, that's me," Michael replied, shaking his hand.

"What are you doing here?" Eu asked.

"I'm a sucker for rehabilitating animals, so I own this place with a partner. You been staying out of trouble since I saw you last, young lady?" Benz asked Eu.

"Not even remotely, and now that I think of it, you may be able to answer a couple of questions for me," Eu replied.

Benz leaned back to sit on the edge of his desk and motioned for them to come in. "Sure, kiddo, what's up?"

"Do you know Josiah Hessel?" Eu asked.

"That boy is trouble from the word go. You need to stay as far as you can from that mess of a man," Benz replied.

"Yeah, that's kind of what I figured from what I found online. What about Ernie Schmidt? Ring any bells?"

Benz frowned and shook his head. "Nope, that one doesn't sound familiar at all."

"Okay, last one," Eu said. "What about Nigel Morence? He owns a boat named The Sandpiper."

"Heard of him, yeah. All positive as far as I remember. What are you up to this time, Miss Eugenia?" Benz asked.

"All sorts of shenanigans, as usual." Eu smiled.

"I suspected as much. You'd better keep a close eye on this one, Professor."

Michael gazed at Eu with a look she hadn't seen before. "Oh, believe me, I do," he said.

Eu blushed and turned toward the door. "I think we should go feed the sloths now. We don't want to miss our time slot," she said, hearing Michael's footsteps behind her as she headed into the hall. "Thanks for the info, Benz!"

"Anytime, Eu. Y'all have fun!"

Within a matter of minutes, Eu was gazing into the trusting eyes of one of the cutest creatures she'd ever seen, while listening to their tour guide pump them full of information about sloths. The baby's arms were wrapped around Eu's neck as she cradled the tiny creature. She looked over at Michael, who was similarly smitten with the sloth that he held ever so gently.

"I don't suppose you loan these out to help people manage stress, do you?" Eu said with a chuckle.

"Aren't they serene?" the guide replied.

"The best." Michael nodded.

They cooed at, petted, and played with the babies until the guide said that it was time for them to go back to their mothers. Neither Eu nor Michael wanted to give them back, but they handed them over and washed their hands again at the sink.

"How can I even begin to thank you for this?" Eu

asked, linking her arm through Michael's as they headed back to the car.

He gazed down at her and smiled. "The look on your face when you were holding the sloth was all the thanks I could ever need. Lunch?"

"Yep, I'm starving!"

CHAPTER TEN

Michael pulled into a sprawling parking lot in front of a restaurant that looked like an oversized beach cabana.

"What is this place?"

"It's a restaurant on the beach. We can eat in chairs with our feet in the water if you'd like."

"That sounds perfect."

They walked through a gift shop to get to the covered patio and then the beach beyond it. Children played in the water while adults looked on, sipping at tropical drinks or having lunch, while a steel drum band played on a covered stage in the distance.

"I can't believe this," Eu exclaimed. "If this was a bay, rather than a lake, I'd swear I was in the Caribbean."

"The food is great too," Michael replied, setting two low sturdy plastic Adirondack chairs into the edge of the cove, while Eu removed her shoes.

"I can't wait. Any recommendations?" she asked, easing into one of the chairs. "Oh, this feels so good, that nice cool water between my toes." She eased back.

"They have a really good seafood platter where you can basically try everything. We could get one and split it. They can do it either grilled or fried and it's more than enough food for two if you order an appetizer," Michael suggested.

"Yes, let's do that, definitely. I think grilled sounds good – do you have a preference?" Eu asked, as Michael made little splashes in the water with his feet.

"I like the grilled one best, so that works out well. They also have a really good spinach artichoke dip that they serve with pretzel bites."

"Two of my all-time favorite things, let's do it!" Eu agreed, thinking this was, without a doubt, one of the best days she'd had in a very long time.

"I'll go order the food and a couple of drinks at the bar and they'll bring it out to us. What would you like to drink?" Michael asked.

"Surprise me," Eu said, shielding her eyes with

her hand as she gazed up at him. "Let me grab my credit card," she said, starting to reach into her pocket.

"Nope, my treat. I'll be right back," he replied, leaving before she could protest.

When he returned a few minutes later, he was carrying two tropical drinks that were so heavily decorated with fruit that Eu didn't know if they'd even need the appetizer, and he had a tall red flag with a number on it tucked under his arm. He handed Eu her drink.

"Thanks for the fruit salad," she teased. "And why are you carrying a flag?"

"You're welcome. The 'fruit salad' is a Tropicolada, and the flag is so they'll know where to bring our lunch." He planted the flag between the backs of their chairs and sat down with his drink.

"What a fun place," Eu said, then took a sip of her drink. "Oh, that's delicious!"

"Yes it is, but you might want to take it slowly," Michael warned, munching on a triangle of pineapple. "So, are you planning on telling me why you were asking Benz all those questions at the park?" he asked casually.

Eu filled him in on everything she'd discovered during her search for Trixie's sister, and he listened attentively, nodding every now and then. Just as she finished speaking, a server came out carrying a table in one hand, which he placed in front of their chairs in the water, and a giant platter of food that included their appetizer and entrée in the other.

"Wow, that's a lot of food." Eu's eyes widened. She was beginning to experience a lovely side effect from her drink, warming her from head to toe and making her feel positively dreamy.

"Let's dig in, then," Michael replied, dipping a pretzel bite into the dip. "So, from what you're telling me, it sounds like you could be putting yourself in danger. I mean, it's admirable how much you care and want to help, but don't you think these unsavory types should be dealt with by the police?" he asked.

Eu cocked her head to the side, a giant shrimp in her hand, and gave him a look. "Really? You know how well Frick and Frack tend to handle these things. And besides, this is Trixie's sister we're talking about, and she's really nice."

"That's fair." Michael nodded. "But when you want to go investigate things, all you have to do is come knock on my door for backup."

Eu swallowed her shrimp and smiled at him. "You'd do that for me?"

"There are quite a few things I'd do for you,"

Michael said lightly, catching her gaze and making her blush to the roots of her hair.

"Is that so? Well then, do you want to go for a hike with me tomorrow?" she asked, her Tropicolada making her bold.

"More than anything." Michael grinned and popped a chunk of lobster into his mouth.

CHAPTER ELEVEN

Michael knocked on Eu's door shortly after sunrise, with two freshly prepared oat milk lattes in hand.

"Those smell amazing," Eu said, inhaling deeply. "Is that just regular coffee?"

"Nope, I made lattes. I hope you like oat milk," Michael replied, following her inside.

"It's my favorite, so this'll be a real treat. I just finished wrapping up some of the lemon bars that were left, so I'll stash them in my backpack, and we can get going," Eu said.

"Great. Where are we headed?" Michael asked, snagging a lemon bar and taking a big bite.

"To the spot where I saw the blood," Eu said quietly.

Michael swallowed and gazed at her. "You know

that sometimes people shoot first and ask questions later around here, right?"

"Yep, I'm aware. You chickening out on me, Professor?" Eu teased.

Michael's gaze was steady. "I'm not worried about *me*."

"Look, I've done some pretty bizarre things to get myself out of trouble since I've been here, so believe me, I know how to be careful by now." Eu smiled.

Michael shook his head. "Just like your mother," he said.

"What's that supposed to mean?" Eu cocked her head to the side and looked up at him.

"Brave and stubborn." Michael laughed, then put the rest of his lemon bar in his mouth. "Let's do this, then."

They nonchalantly strolled across the parking lot toward the marina, then went up the hill and disappeared into the woods, making a beeline for the spot where Eu had seen the blood.

They were nearing the area when Michael stopped short, putting out a hand so that Eu would as well and putting a finger to his lips. He inclined his head toward a spot in the trees up ahead and Eu saw a rather wild-haired woman crouching by a tree. They exchanged a look and silently moved closer.

"Hello there," Eu called out softly, having no idea what they'd just stumbled into.

The woman jumped and whirled to face them, a basket of something flying out of her hands.

"Good gawd a'mighty! You can't just come up on a person and scare the daylights out of 'em like that!" she said, glancing furtively toward the house at the top of the hill.

"I'm really sorry, I just saw you crouched down and wanted to make sure you were okay," Eu said.

"Of course I'm hunkered down, ya can't hunt morels standing up straight," the woman replied, hands on hips.

"Morels? You mean like mushrooms? They have those here? They're a delicacy," Eu exclaimed, her mouth watering.

"They ain't easy to find. I could sell you some, but it ain't gonna be cheap," the woman said eyes narrowed shrewdly.

"How much for the whole basket?" Michael asked.

"Quite a bit, and you'd have to pick 'em up yourselves since you made me drop 'em."

"Consider it done." Michael walked over, haggled for a few seconds, then paid her and started picking up the mushrooms.

Eu spotted a scrap of fabric on a nearby tree. Making sure that no one was looking, she took it down and pocketed it.

"Do you live around here?" she asked the mushroom seller.

The woman stared at her, clearly suspicious. "Why?"

"Oh, I just wondered. I heard a scream close to here the other day, and I wondered if you might know anything about what happened," Eu said, widening her eyes to look more innocent.

"Yeah, I know what happened. I acted like a dang school girl when I saw a snake. I screamed and ran. Scraped the heck out of my knee on that stump over there." She pointed to where Eu had found the blood.

Eu looked down at the woman's legs and sure enough, there was a nasty looking scrape wound.

"Oh, I don't blame you a bit. I hate snakes." Eu shuddered. "Have you seen any today?" she asked.

"Couple." She shrugged. "Now, I ain't got time to chit chat, I gotta find more of these morels since I didn't keep any for myself yet."

"Well, good luck. Hope you don't see any snakes," Eu said.

The woman grunted a reply and walked away, scanning the ground ahead.

"Shall we?" Michael asked, closing Eu's backpack after filling it with morels. He looked toward the marina.

"Yeah, I guess so." Eu sighed. "Are you afraid of snakes?"

"They're not my favorite animal, but I've had good luck with them by keeping a respectful distance."

"Fair warning, my idea of keeping a respectful distance is sprinting away as fast as possible," Eu replied.

"I'll keep an eye out," Michael said, a corner of his mouth lifting in what looked like a suppressed smile. "Well, this trip was helpful. At least it's good to know it wasn't Trixie's sister who left the blood trail."

"Yes, that's true, but she might have left this," Eu said, pulling the scrap of fabric she'd found out of her pocket.

CHAPTER TWELVE

Shortly after Eu woke up, Fran called, demanding to hear all about her date with Michael. Eu filled her in on all the details, including their lunch on the water.

"Wow, he hit that one out of the park," Fran said, chuckling.

"It was so much fun," Eu agreed.

"See, I told you he liked you," Fran replied in a singsong voice.

"Oh, stop. I think I'm very much in the friend zone," Eu said, her heart rate speeding up nonetheless at the thought that Michael might be interested.

"And that, my dear, is your fault. Gotta let him know you have a crush on him," Fran replied.

"He's having me over for steak and morels for

lunch – it's going to be so delicious," Eu said, glad that Fran couldn't see her blushing.

"Perfect chance to tell him how you feel," Fran prodded.

"I'll feel like eating steak, that's how I'll feel." Eu laughed.

"Better lure him in or I might cast my line in that pond," Fran teased.

"You're incorrigible."

"That's why we're besties."

"Absolutely." Eu laughed. "I have to go work on my article now. Gotta support myself, you know."

"Yeah, sure. Way to avoid the conversation. Okay, fine, go work on your article, but I want a full report on the steak date."

"It's not a date."

"Make it one."

Eu hung up laughing and was still smiling as she grabbed her laptop to work on her article.

She had the best of intentions, she really did, but as Eu stared at the blank computer screen, with her cursor blinking accusingly at her, her mind kept wandering to Trixie's missing sister. Finally accepting the fact that she wasn't going to be productive, she decided to go for a walk near the marina that was behind her cabin for a change of scenery.

Enjoying the sun baking into her exposed skin while listening to the lapping of the lake as it gently flowed to and from the shore, Eu skirted around the docks of the marina and was about to enter the woods on the other side, when something stuck in a bit of underbrush and flapping in the light breeze caught her attention.

Crouching next to the spot where she'd seen the paper, Eu looked carefully for wildlife before reaching out and delicately plucking what turned out to be a brochure. A brochure that just happened to be from the RV park where Trixie's ex lived. It still had good color, so it likely hadn't been out in the weather for long, and when Eu turned it over, examining each side, she saw a phone number scrawled on the back.

"This can't be just a coincidence," she murmured. Trixie might not think that her ex was capable of nefarious plots, but Eu wasn't so sure. "I wonder who'll answer this number."

Pocketing the brochure, she turned back and strode toward her cabin to do more investigating. Once inside, she dialed the number on the brochure and heard a tinny voice informing her that the number was no longer in service. Frustrated, she made a note of the street address of the RV park and looked up individual addresses until she finally found one with Trixie's last name.

"Well, it looks like I'm going to go see Ernie Schmidt," Eu decided.

Before she could change her mind, she set out on foot, headed for the RV park that was only a couple of miles away. What she hadn't calculated as part of her plan was that the RV park was two *Ozark* miles away. Which meant up and down some serious hills, walking on a twelve inch strip of packed gravel along the side of the road, as massive trucks pulling boats, and minivans filled with tourists, whizzed by so closely that her hair blew into her face. And somehow, the sun along the road was hotter, bearing down on her head and shoulders like a thick, stuffy blanket.

By the time she got to the RV park, Eu was tired, sweaty, and fairly certain there might be a small blister on the back of her heel. She stopped for a moment when she arrived, leaning against a stone pillar to the side of the driveway into the park, catching her breath in a tiny patch of shade.

"Okay, here we go."

Eu walked along in front of the RV spaces, looking for Ernie Schmidt's number and giggling to herself when she thought about asking if he lived with

Bert. "The heat must be getting to me," she said, shaking her head.

She found Ernie's RV, which was clearly a permanent residence. There was a gravel path leading to a porch that was covered by a green and white striped awning. Somewhere in the distance, a windchime made lovely sounds, notes ringing out on a soft, merciful breeze.

Eu rang the doorbell and manufactured a smile when an older man, with a scar running down the entire left side of his face from forehead to chin, answered the door. He was tall, with thin arms and legs and a belly that suggested he liked to eat. Ernie wore a shapeless navy colored t-shirt and jeans that had seen better days.

His eyes lit up with an interest that Eu didn't even want to think about. "Yeah?" he said, his accent thick enough to be heard, even in the utterance of that one simple word.

"Hi, are you Ernie?" she asked, her smile still saccharin.

He leaned against the doorframe, folded his arms and looked Eu over, from head to toe and back again. Eu wanted to shudder but kept smiling.

"Who wants to know?" he asked, seeming interested, but wary.

"Well, I do, That's why I'm here." Eu went for a doe-eyed expression.

"I'm Ernie and I don't know you, so how 'bout you state your business, girl," he replied.

"Sure, I don't want to impose," Eu said, somehow managing to maintain a sweet expression though her face hurt from forcing it. "My friend Bella is visiting, and she told me she was going to go see some people she knew in the area and she mentioned you, so I was wondering if she had dropped by," she continued.

"Ain't nobody by that name been around here," Ernie replied. "So, unless you're fixin' to come in here and make me a sandwich, you best be on your way, little girl."

Eu wanted to throw something at him. "Haha, that's funny. Okay, well, thanks anyway," she said instead, giving him a coy wave.

Ernie Schmidt quickly stepped back into his RV and closed the door in her face. Eu grimaced.

She trotted down the porch steps and spotted something that made her stomach do a nervous little flip. Darting her eyes toward Ernie's windows to make sure he wasn't watching her, she hurried over to a hedge that stood between Ernie's lot and the one to his left.

She bent down and picked up a wrapper that was stuck between two of the hedge's thin branches.

"Caramel Cluster," she whispered, the color draining from her face when she realized that Bella had said that particular candy bar was her favorite. Heart pounding, Eu stuck the wrapper in her pocket and hurried away from Ernie's RV, keeping her eyes open for any other possible clues.

By the time she got back to the cabin, she was dehydrated and exhausted.

"Okay, water first, then I'll sit down in this wonderfully air-conditioned cabin and write my article once and for all."

Despite her good intentions, after downing more than thirty-two ounces of vitamin and mineral-infused water, Eu decided to sit on the couch and close her eyes for a moment. When the sound of a speedboat startled her awake, she realized that she only had half an hour to get ready for her steak lunch with Michael.

After practically sprinting through the shower, Eu decided to dress casually and only wear the faintest traces of makeup. She definitely didn't want to make it appear that she was trying too hard to get Michael's attention. Putting on a pair of small gold hoop earrings and adding just a spritz of perfume, she slid her feet into cute but practical sandals and headed over.

The smell of steak on the grill tantalized her before she even got to the door, and her stomach growled in anticipation.

"Hey, perfect timing," Michael said when he opened the door. "The steaks are about ready to come off the grill and everything else is done too," he explained, standing back to welcome her into his cabin.

"It smells so amazing in here," Eu said, inhaling a buffet of aromas as he shut the door behind her. "Is there anything I can do to help?"

"Yes, if you could grab the bottle of wine that's on the table and pour both of us a glass, that would be great. It'll pair perfectly with the steak and sides."

"I like the sound of that." Eu grinned and headed for the table.

She poured the wine, taking a tiny sip to taste it, and was pleasantly surprised at the depth and nuance of it. She sighed with contentment, closing her eyes briefly.

"Glad you like it. It's one of my favorites," Michael said, setting a platter of steak and a side dish of morels on the table.

"I can't even read the label." Eu frowned.

Michael chuckled. "It's French."

"I feel so sophisticated now," Eu said, picking up her wine with exaggerated flair and sticking out her pinkie before taking another sip. She swallowed and laughed, cracking Michael up. "So, where's Callie? Is she late?" Eu asked.

Michael set a dish of buttery herbed baby potatoes and a tray of grilled asparagus on the table. "Nope, I didn't invite her," he replied casually.

Eu dramatically put her wrist to her brow and affected a southern belle voice. "Well, Professor Michael, I do declare… Whatever will people think of the two of us alone in here consuming food together?" She fanned herself, pretending to feel faint.

Michael grinned. "I don't really care what people think, do you?"

"I suppose I can risk my honor and reputation for a spoonful of those morels," Eu replied in her belle voice.

They both laughed.

The food was nothing short of spectacular. Eu told Michael that if he ever got tired of teaching Physics, he could certainly become a chef.

"Some days that's tempting," he replied. "So,

what trouble have you gotten in so far today?" he asked.

"You know me too well." Eu smiled. She told him about the candy bar wrapper she'd found near Ernie's RV, and that she needed to check with Trixie to see if the scrap of fabric that she'd found belonged to anything that Bella might have worn.

Michael nodded, cutting a perfectly cooked piece of steak. "Okay, but let's think this through for a second. If the fabric was found in the woods, near Josiah's house, but the brochure was found across the peninsula near the other marina, and Trixie's ex lives in the RV park on the brochure, how would a piece of Bella's clothing be found in one place and info from Ernie in another?"

Eu savored a bite of steak with morel as she considered his point. "Well, I don't know. Maybe he came to the other marina by boat, then walked across the parking lot up here and went into the woods."

"It's possible. Maybe he works for Nigel Morence and borrowed the Sandpiper to impress Bella. She goes aboard to see the boat, and he takes off fast, so she's trapped with him."

A shiver went up Eu's spine and she nodded, munching on a baby asparagus spear. "That's a pretty good theory, Professor. Want to rent a boat tomorrow?"

"Somehow, I knew you were going to ask that," Michael said with a smile. "But why wait? If we're going on a stealth mission, why not go tonight, after dark? I know the lake well enough to navigate with running lights."

CHAPTER THIRTEEN

"Well, this isn't creepy at all," Eu muttered, reaching for Michael's hand as he helped her onto the boat in the darkness.

"It'll be beautiful when we get out onto the water," Michael promised, guiding her to the passenger seat.

"I'm sure that's what they thought in Friday the 13th too," Eu said, arching an eyebrow at him.

Michael chuckled. "That's just a movie, Eu."

"Yeah, well fine, but the Loch Ness Monster is real," Eu shot back, glad she'd worn jeans and a sweatshirt as she sank back into the cool leather seat.

"That's debatable, but even if it is real, it's in Ireland, so we don't need to worry about it," Michael replied.

"Do you even know how to drive this thing?" Eu asked, gripping the armrest.

"Nope, but I'm a professor, remember? So, I'm sure I can figure it out," he teased.

"Wait...seriously?"

"Eu, relax. I've got this, okay? I've driven boats almost as much as I've driven cars. We'll be fine," Michael assured her.

"I'm sorry. I just don't have much experience around boats. My dad and I always fished from the shore. I see you got a dark colored one," Eu said, trying her best to sound positive. "That was good thinking."

"Yep, the motor is nearly silent too, and I figured once we get close, I can cut the lights and we'll just glide up alongside the Sandpiper to check things out," Michael said, starting the engine and backing out of the slip as it purred along.

Eu shivered.

"Do you need a coat? I brought an extra just in case, and some blankets too," Michael said.

Eu sighed. "No, I'm fine. I just have this weird feeling."

"Understandable." Michael gave her a reassuring smile. "Being on the water at night for the first time can be like that. Just try to relax and enjoy it. Chances are quite good that we're not going to find anything anyway, so then we can just have a smooth cruise back."

Eu took a deep breath and nodded. Relax. Sure.

Fortunately, Michael was right. As the sizable boat skimmed nearly silently across the lake, which was like glass in the stillness of night, Eu began to enjoy the feel of the breeze on her face and the sight of Michael expertly piloting them through the moonlight.

After about half an hour of what was turning out to be a lovely ride, Michael throttled the engine back and slowed the boat. "Based on the address you found, the Sandpiper should be in the marina just around that bend," he said, pointing out into an area speckled with lights.

"What if someone sees us?" Eu asked.

Michael shrugged, almost infuriatingly unconcerned. Nothing seemed to rattle that man. Eu liked that about him. "Then we tell them we rented a boat and got lost. They'll just think we're dumb tourists and send us on our way."

"Oh. That totally makes sense. Good plan."

"I have my moments." He chuckled.

Michael glided carefully into a slip between two boats that were decidedly larger than the one they were in, and Eu stepped out to secure the lines as he cut the engine. It was so quiet they could hear the lapping of the waves against the dock that had been created by their wake. They started down the dock, looking for the Sandpiper, and heard another noise. One that gave Eu shivers. First, a knocking sound, followed by a muffled cry. They stopped moving and listened. The sound came to them again, a knocking, then the cries.

"Look, there's the Sandpiper," Eu whispered, pointing.

"And that's where the sounds are coming from," Michael replied grimly, hurrying toward the boat with Eu at his heels.

The sounds got louder.

"We have to go aboard," Eu whispered.

Michael nodded and helped her climb up, then followed after.

They inched toward the sounds, which were coming from below the deck of the fairly large boat.

Eu had just stepped down the first step to go below deck, when a bright light washed over the marina from the water. "Michael, behind you!" Eu screamed.

A dark figure was closing in fast.

Michael turned and tackled his would-be

assailant, getting him to the ground and pinning his arms in a manner so efficient that Eu was both surprised and impressed.

"I've got this. Go see what's happening," Michael encouraged.

Eu hurried down the stairs, where the sounds had grown more frantic.

"Shhh. It's okay. You're safe now, Bella. We've got you," Eu said, feeling along the walls for a light.

When she found a switch, she flipped it on. There was a woman, bound, gagged, and terrified, but it definitely wasn't Bella.

CHAPTER FOURTEEN

Eu went to the clearly terrified woman, who was huddled in the corner of a bunk bed. She first untied her wrists and feet, then removed a gag that had been fashioned out of a bandana and helped her toward the door.

Eu was more than relieved to discover that the bright light had come from a Coast Guard boat with a crew that had been suspicious after spotting them dousing their lights and cruising into the marina. When the Coast Guard crew jumped onto the dock, Michael, still holding a man down, explained why they were there, as Eu helped the woman slowly up the stairs.

One of the crew quickly took over, wrapping a blanket around the victim and walking her down the dock to board the Coast Guard boat. Eu trailed behind them and before the rescued woman stepped across to board, she thanked Eu profusely and asked for her phone number. The seemingly ever prepared Coast Guard member pulled a small notebook out of his shirt pocket, as well as a pen, and handed them to Eu. She wrote her number on one of the pages, tore it out, and gave it to the woman, telling her to call or text if she needed a friend.

When she was safely aboard, Eu turned back to see two other crew members putting zip ties on the kidnapper's hands and feet. Since they were impounding the boat for evidence, they dragged him aboard and followed the Coast Guard boat out of the marina in the Sandpiper.

Eu, shaking like a leaf now that the worst was over, threw herself into Michael's arms. "That was so brave, I was so worried about you," she blurted, as her cheek rested against his chest, safely encircled in his arms.

"Thanks. You were pretty brave yourself, Eugenia," he said, gazing down at her, an unfathomable look in his eyes. "Ready to go home?" he asked.

Eu nodded, the rush of emotions surging through her too complicated to even try to figure out.

CHAPTER FIFTEEN

"Hey Trixie, I wanted to show you something and I hope you don't get too upset," Eu said, hurrying to the front counter at the general store.

"Well, you certainly have my attention." Trixie's brows rose and she closed the magazine she was reading.

Eu reached into her pocket, brought out the piece of fabric that she'd found, and handed it to Trixie.

"Does this look like something that belongs to Bella?" Eu asked gently.

Trixie smiled and shook her head. "Yeah, that's hers alright, that little numbskull." She barked out a raspy laugh.

Eu's mouth dropped open and she stared at Trixie.

Trixie laughed again. "I shoulda had my phone

out to take a picture of your face. I guess you haven't heard yet. That dang sister of mine got spooked by a sound in the woods, took off running, and got herself lost. Some forest rangers found her about fifteen miles from here, scared to death and hoarding one last candy bar." She shook her head.

Eu nearly wilted with relief. "Oh, thank goodness that's all it was. Is she okay?" she asked.

"Yep, she's fine, just hungry and shook up. Thanks for all your hard work though, Nancy Drew." Trixie winked.

Eu laughed. "Well, I didn't really do anything helpful, and I am so done with mysteries."

"I heard you were a hero who found a kidnapped woman," Trixie said, eyeing her with something that looked like admiration. "They put that evil so and so in jail, and I'm guessing he ain't gonna get out anytime soon."

"Thank goodness for that. I'm glad I had Michael with me. He tackled him and held him there until the Coast Guard came," Eu replied.

"I'll bet you're glad he went along." Trixie gave her a sly grin.

Eu blushed but was spared from replying when a text came in, interrupting the conversation with a loud ding. "I need to take this," she said, hurrying from the store, Trixie's laughter following her out the door.

The text was from a number Eu didn't recognize, but when she opened it and read it, it was from the woman who had been kidnapped. She was sending an invitation to Eu to meet her for lunch at The Chateau – a swanky restaurant nearby.

Eu texted back that she'd be delighted to join her for lunch and immediately began stressing out over what to wear. Her Ozarks wardrobe didn't really include fashionable items that were suitable for an impromptu luncheon at a bougie restaurant.

"Wait a minute. Callie was a model. I wonder if she could help me," Eu mused. "One way to find out."

She slid her feet into ancient flip flops and headed for Callie's cabin. Callie opened the door half an inch, but when she saw it was Eu, she opened it all the way.

"Hi, I'm really sorry to bother you," Eu blurted. "But I got invited to a lunch at The Chateau today and I have zero nice clothes, but since you were a model and all, I was wondering if you might be able to help me with making the most out of the things that I have?"

Callie smiled. "I can do better than that," she replied. "Come on in."

Eu entered a surprisingly stylish living room and followed Callie down the hall where her guest room would have been. Callie put her hand on the doorknob and turned to Eu. "Are you ready for this?" she asked.

"Um…sure?" Eu said, not sure at all.

Callie opened the door to a room filled with racks of clothing, accessories, shoes, and purses.

Eu gasped.

"Most of the clothing that I modeled, I kept, so there is a ton of vintage stuff in here, but there are also more recent choices, on the rack against that wall." Callie inclined her head toward the left. She went to one of the racks in the middle and pulled out a filmy pink cocktail dress.

"This was your mom's. She was curvier than me, so I can't wear it, but I bet it'd look like a dream on you," Callie said, holding up the stunning dress.

"That was my mom's?" Eu whispered, swallowing past the lump that had formed in her throat. Callie nodded, then came over and handed it to her.

"There's a changing room in the back corner. You should try it on."

Eu held the hanger in one hand and ran her fingers over the gossamer fabric with the other, tears welling in her eyes. Unable to speak, she nodded and moved in the direction that Callie had pointed.

Patting her eyes dry with the t-shirt she removed, Eu gently took her mother's dress from the hanger and undid the zipper and the pearl button at the top of it. She turned her back to the mirror to slip it on, and discovered that Callie had been right, it fit like a dream. She wrapped her arms around her midsection and stared at her reflection for a moment, wondering again about the mother she'd never known.

"Need help zipping it up all the way?" Callie called out softly from beyond the changing room door.

Eu couldn't speak, so she opened the door and nodded.

Callie gasped and a sob caught in her throat. She covered her mouth with her hands and her eyes welled as she stared at Eu. "It's like seeing a ghost," she choked out finally. "A beautiful, beloved ghost."

She lifted her arms and Eu went into them. After a moment, Callie stepped back, her hands on Eu's shoulders. "She loved you so much. She missed you every day. You know that, right?" she whispered.

Eu nodded.

"Honey, every eye in that place is going to be on you when you walk in." Callie smiled, placing her hands on either side of Eu's face. "Now let's find you some accessories."

CHAPTER SIXTEEN

Something that Eu found fascinating happened when she returned home with her mother's dress, shoes, and jewelry and began to get ready. Instead of having the jitters that she normally would have when meeting someone new in an unfamiliar situation, the more steps she took, the more confident she became.

With every stroke of the hairbrush, every touch of makeup, the clicking into place of the clasp on her necklace, and the final rasp of the zipper closing on the back of the dress, Eu felt like she was putting on protective armor to go do battle. And for once in her life, she felt like she was going to a battle that she just might win.

The valet at The Chateau took the keys to

Michael's car and Eu strode to the entrance of the fancy restaurant with her head held high.

She greeted the host with a smile.

"Hello, I'm here to meet Julia," she said, realizing that she'd forgotten to ask the kidnapped woman's last name.

Fortunately, the host knew who she meant and asked her to follow him. He led her to a door so discreet that Eu figured most people wouldn't even notice it.

"Private dining, mademoiselle," the host said, opening the door and gesturing for her to enter.

She thanked him before he closed it behind her. Julia looked much better than she had after being held captive, and she smiled broadly when she saw Eu. Eu smiled back and couldn't help but think that she looked awfully familiar for some reason.

"Eugenia," Julia said, standing to give Eu a hug. "You look beautiful."

"Thanks, so do you," Eu replied, sitting next to her at a round table that was decked out with the finest linens, China, crystal, and silver.

Before Julia could reply, the door opened again, and when Eu saw who entered the room, she gasped. Her mother's sister, her aunt, Mauricia, who had been nothing but nasty to her, glided in, nose in the air, red-eyed, and haggard beneath her expertly applied makeup.

Mauricia froze in her tracks when she spotted Eu sitting with Julia, her icy mask of contempt slipping for a moment.

Eu glanced from Mauricia to Julia, and back again. "Are you two related?" she asked, noting a rather profound resemblance.

Julia nodded, covered Eu's hand with hers for a moment, giving it a little squeeze before letting go. "My mother," she inclined her head toward Mauricia, who still hadn't moved. "I'm your cousin. When you told me your name at the dock, I thought it sounded so familiar, and once I was able to return to reality, I figured it out. You looked like my aunt Miranda. She told me about you." Julia's smile was warm.

Appearing to come to her senses, Mauricia stalked over to the table and stared directly at Julia, ignoring Eu altogether. "You told me that I would be meeting the person who saved your life," she snipped, glaring at her daughter.

"You are," Julia said firmly. "Now sit down, please, Mother. We're going to have lunch."

"I couldn't eat right now if you paid me to," Eu murmured.

"Nor could I," Mauricia said, the ice in her tone causing an almost palpable chill in the elegant room.

"Fine, then we'll just talk," Julia insisted. "The server left us some champagne and I think it'll take the edge off for all of us."

Julia glanced over at a sommelier that Eu hadn't even noticed, who'd apparently been standing in the corner waiting for his cue. With a white linen cloth draped over one arm, he approached the table and filled each glass with champagne.

"Sit please, Mother." Julia gave Mauricia a look. Begrudgingly, the older woman waited for the sommelier to pull out her chair and sat, as far away as she could from Eu.

"Now then, family, let's raise our glasses in a toast," Julia said, raising hers with a smile.

Feeling as though she was on automatic pilot, Eu did the same, and with a sour expression reminiscent of the Grinch if he had particularly bad heartburn, so did Mauricia.

"To new beginnings," Julia said, clinking her glass first against Eu's and then against her mother's.

Eu drank half of her champagne in a couple of gulps and the sommelier refilled her glass without missing a beat.

Julia took a breath and turned to Eu. "Your mom

was the most amazing woman. She was always so kind. If she saw a baby squirrel fall from a tree, she'd be on the phone with the park service while she went out and put a blanket around the poor thing. She was so creative, and always looked amazing, even when she was in her fishing gear. She had this dry sense of humor and could always make us all crack up. The thing that made her so sad was that she couldn't be with you and your dad. No one outside the family knew about you, and she had to keep it that way so that her husband wouldn't find out about you still coming around. He's not a nice guy." She grimaced.

When she stopped talking, Eu, who had silent tears streaming down her face, heard a sound and glanced over at Mauricia, who was dabbing at her eyes with a designer handkerchief.

Taking her chin a notch higher, Mauricia took a breath and seemingly reigned in her emotions. She focused on Eu, staring intently for so long, that Eu was wondering if she was having some kind of episode.

"I blamed you, you know, for your mother never reaching her full potential," Mauricia said.

Julia snorted most inelegantly and turned to Eu. "Don't let my mother fool you. Miranda was quite an accomplished artist. Her work sold for millions in the global market," she explained.

Mauricia made a face. "She knows all that. She inherited every last dime of Miranda's money."

Eu's head was beginning to feel a bit fuzzy, for all sorts of reasons. "Ummm… What money?" she asked, frowning.

Mauricia's brows rose so high that Eu wondered if they might float away like an errant balloon. "She left you everything that she had earned from her art, including her studio in Manhattan. How can you not know this?" she demanded.

"How could I possibly have known that? It's not like you told me," Eu replied, reeling at the revelation. Then a thought occurred to her.

"The clue!" She blurted, leaping to her feet. "The one clue that made no sense! Now I know." She laughed.

"This has been good, but I need to excuse myself," she said.

Julia hugged her hard, like she didn't want to let go. "We're going to keep in touch," she whispered. "I'm glad there's still such a big part of your mom in this world."

Eu squeezed her back and thanked her, then turned to go.

"Eugenia," Mauricia said quietly.

Eu instantly sobered and gazed at her aunt without speaking, bracing herself for an acidic parting gift.

"Eugenia, I apologize. I assumed that you were something that you clearly were not, and I wish you well. I think perhaps I was merely jealous of you because my sister loved you so much more than she did me." Mauricia's lower lip quivered momentarily.

"But you'll always have something that I never will," Eu replied, tears in her eyes. She took her aunt's hand. "You got to know her, hug her, hear her laugh. Nothing can ever take that away."

Julia's voice came softly from the other side of the table. "I have some home movies that I'll copy and send to you. I know it won't be the same as being with her, but you'll at least be able to hear her voice."

Unable to speak, Eu nodded. Mauricia's hand dropped from hers. "I wish you only the best, Eugenia. I truly do. I just need some time to process."

Eu nodded again and headed for the exit.

CHAPTER SEVENTEEN

Still wearing her mother's dress and jewelry, Eu went immediately to her walk-in closet, peeled back the carpet, and lifted the wooden floor planks beneath it up, revealing one of her mother's hiding places, where she'd squirreled away paintings, painting supplies, and other personal treasures that hadn't made sense to Eu before now.

One of the items in the hiding place was a key that Eu had found under her bed. It was small, and she'd been puzzling for months about why the key had been there and what it might unlock. On the back were the letters NBO and the numbers 017. The key had to go to a safety deposit box, so Eu looked up the name of every bank in the area and found the National Bank of the Ozarks. NBO. What the 017 meant, she didn't know, but she hoped she'd find out when she went to the bank.

After changing into shorts and a sleeveless polo shirt, Eu borrowed Michael's car with a quick, 'I'll tell you why later.' She pulled up directions to the bank on her phone and headed directly there. When she walked in the door, the teller, who looked old enough to be Eu's mother, stared at Eu like she'd seen a ghost.

"Hi," Eu said, approaching the counter. "I'm…"

Before she could finish her sentence, the teller interrupted her.

"Oh, darlin,' I know who you are. You look just like your sweet mama, rest her soul. Come with me, sweetie," she said, coming out from behind the counter and walking briskly toward a large brass door.

The teller typed in a code on a box next to the door, and after a series of metallic clanks, it swung open. "Come on in, hon," the teller said, leading Eu into a room that reminded her a bit of a mausoleum. There were richly wood paneled walls lined with locked drawers. "You got your key, or do you need another one?" the teller asked.

"I have this," Eu said, holding up the small key.

"Yep, that's it. The numbers are backwards. Your

mama's box is in number 710." She pointed out the drawer. "I'll let you have some privacy. You just push that white button next to the door when you're ready to leave, okay? There's a security bag in the drawer if you'd like to remove any or all of the items in your drawer."

"Thank you," Eu murmured, her eyes fixed on the drawer.

She went to the drawer and traced her fingers over the numbers, both eager and reluctant to open it. Everything that her mother wanted her to have or to know, was in that drawer. She wished she had her father at her side so that he could share the moment with her. The thought brought tears to her eyes. Her mother loved her, according to everyone who had known her, which made Eu happy and grateful beyond belief, but it was still a lot to take in.

"I'm about to meet you, Mom," she whispered, sliding the small key into the lock, silent tears sliding down her cheeks.

There were all sorts of official documents in the drawer. Deeds to multiple properties, bank account information, investments, and a jewelry box filled to the brim with sparkling treasures. But Eu found what she was really looking for underneath the documents and the jewelry box.

There, against the rich velvet liner of the drawer, was a well-worn diary. In the front cover of the diary was an envelope with her name on it. As she took the envelope out of the diary with shaking fingers, Eu noticed that the first entry in the diary was dated a couple of years before she was born. Doodles and happy sayings in handwriting that was eerily like her own covered the front cover of the diary. It made Eu smile, but her expression grew serious when she turned the envelope with her name on it over and over in her hands.

From beyond the grave, her mother was reaching out to her. Inside the envelope were undoubtedly words meant for her from the mother she never knew.

"Why am I scared?" she whispered, her hands and voice shaking. Eu sat in a velvet upholstered chair in the corner and opened the flap of the envelope, taking out a letter. She clutched it in both hands and held it to her heart for a moment, her tears flowing freely.

Taking some deep breaths, she gingerly opened the letter as if it would disintegrate if she handled it too roughly.

My dearest Eugenia,

I am so sorry, my darling girl. I didn't want to leave you. Ever. You and your dad were the best things that ever happened to me, and I've missed you every day since I saw you for the last time. You held your daddy's hand and cried for me as you left. My heart broke into a million pieces that day, and I don't know that it ever recovered.

I knew I would never love again the way that I love you and your father, so I found my joy in nature, and in painting, and in helping others... and in stolen moments far away from a world that I would never have asked to be born into.

None of this was your fault. Please know that you weren't abandoned. You were so loved. ARE so loved. I cry for you every day my sweet girl.

I know that material things can't make up for the time we could never share together, but I hope I can at least make some things easier for you, now that you're an adult. I'm so proud of you, Eugenia. I know you'll be able to handle whatever life throws your way. I've been watching you from afar and I love the person you've become.

I've recorded the most important things in my life in the pages of my diary, including my daily thoughts of the family I should have had. I mourn in these pages. I breathe and live in these pages. My heart beats in these pages.

My gift to you is the absolute knowledge that with every breath I took, from the moment we met in the delivery room, you were precious to me. All that I did, I did to keep you safe and well. I hope one day you'll understand.

I love you more than life, dear Eugenia. The day that your hair ribbon stopped smelling like your silky sweet toddler hair, I felt a loss as deep as death. Please live the life that you want to live, the life that you deserve. I didn't have that chance, but it's all I want for you, my beloved daughter.

Be free to love, and don't be afraid.

Your mother, always. Miranda

CHAPTER EIGHTEEN

The feeling of déjà vu was overwhelming when Eu and Michael pulled up in front of the small house in Los Angeles that she used to share with Fran. It was evening, but not late enough for Fran to have gone out, and Eu's heart pounded with excitement.

"Hey, bestie," Eu said with a mischievous grin when Fran opened the door.

Fran flew into her arms, hugging her like she'd never let go, babbling about being shocked and needing to clean the house before having company. After releasing Eu, she squealed like a kid with a new toy and hugged Michael, then dragged them both inside.

"Okay, you two knocked my socks off with your surprise, now, what gives?" Fran demanded, bouncing up and down on the ottoman in front of Eu's favorite overstuffed chair. "Tell me everything."

"You might want to break out some wine for this conversation," Eu said.

When they were all sipping on a fabulous cabernet that Fran had been saving for a special occasion, Eu told the story of her mother and read her letter aloud. There wasn't a dry eye in the room when she finished, and Fran climbed into the oversized chair with her best friend, hugging her tightly.

"Oh, honey. I'm so happy for you. I mean, sad, but happy, if that makes sense," Fran said, sniffling. Michael handed them each a tissue and took one for himself.

Eu laughed through her tears and nodded. "Yeah, I definitely get that. I was such a mess after I opened the bank box that I had to sit in the car for a while before I could drive."

Fran leaned her head on Eu's shoulder. "I bet," she said, taking a sip of wine. "It's not even my letter and I'm going to need to sleep with a cucumber mask on my eyes tonight," she joked. "So, now that you're a member of the rich and shameless, what are you going to do with your life? Are you coming back to L.A?"

"Actually, I think I'm going to open up a

publishing company in this cute little Midwest college town that I've heard so much about," Eu said, gazing fondly at Michael.

"I knew it! I knew you two would get together at some point. This is fabulous – congratulations you sly dogs," Fran teased. "Are you going to keep your mom's cabin?"

"Absolutely! And you can use it anytime you'd like, but you have to promise to do the dishes every once in a while." Eu grinned.

Fran glanced over at the sink full of dishes that seemed to mock her from the kitchen. "Or maybe I'll just hire that out," she said, chuckling. "So, you two crazy kids, are there wedding bells in the future?" She batted her eyes. "I've been dying to be your bridesmaid."

Eu blushed and Michael laughed.

"One step at a time, Fran. One step at a time," her best friend forever said, raising her glass.

ALSO BY SUMMER PRESCOTT

Check out all the books in Summer Prescott's catalog!

Summer Prescott Book Catalog

AUTHOR'S NOTE

I'd love to hear your thoughts on my books, the storylines, and anything else that you'd like to comment on—reader feedback is very important to me. My contact information, along with some other helpful links, is listed on the next page. If you'd like to be on my list of "folks to contact" with updates, release and sales notifications, etc.… just shoot me an email and let me know. Thanks for reading!

Also…

… if you're looking for more great reads, Summer Prescott Books publishes several popular series by outstanding Cozy Mystery authors.

CONTACT SUMMER PRESCOTT BOOKS PUBLISHING

Twitter: @summerprescott1

Bookbub: https://www.bookbub.com/authors/summer-prescott

Blog and Book Catalog: http://summerprescottbooks.com

Email: summer.prescott.cozies@gmail.com

YouTube: https://www.youtube.com/channel/UCngKNUkDdWuQ5k7-Vkfrp6A

And…be sure to check out the Summer Prescott Cozy Mysteries fan page and Summer Prescott Books Publishing Page on Facebook – let's be friends!

To download a free book, and sign up for our fun and exciting newsletter, which will give you opportunities to win prizes and swag, enter contests, and be the first to know about New Releases, click here: http://summerprescottbooks.com

Printed in Great Britain
by Amazon